Tanya Routh.

JAN WAHL
Sylvester Bear Overslept

pictures by LEE LORENZ

Parents' Magazine Press • *New York*

Text copyright © 1979 by Jan Wahl. Illustrations copyright © 1979 by Lee Lorenz.
All rights reserved. Printed in the United States of America
10 9 8 7 6 5 4 3 2 1

Library of Congress Cataloging in Publication Data

Wahl, Jan.   Sylvester Bear overslept.
Summary: Sylvester Bear desperately wants to escape his wife's snoring but
soon realizes it is truly music to his ears.
[1. Snoring—Fiction. 2. Sleep—Fiction. 3. Bears—Fiction]
I. Lorenz, Lee. II. Title. PZ7.W1266Sy   [E]   79-4095
ISBN 0-8193-1003-4   ISBN 0-8193-1004-2 lib. bdg.

For Bert, warmly   (J.W.)
For Nicholas   (L. L.)

The sky was silver.
Yellow-orange maple leaves were falling.
Winter would soon be here.

At the edge of the woods, in a cozy cottage,
lived Sylvester Bear and his wife Phyllis.

Sylvester was in the apple tree
shaking apples.
"Soon it will be time for our
winter nap," said Phyllis.
"I know. But before we sleep,
we must eat," said Sylvester.

They carried the apples into the kitchen
where Sylvester peeled and cored them.
Phyllis rolled out dough and shook sugar
and cinnamon and a pinch of salt
over the apples.

In an hour or two they had baked
thirty-five pies.

Together they ate all thirty-five.

Phyllis watched the clock.
"It's getting late, Sylvester."
"I know," he replied.
He gave her a hug and she gave him one.
Then they said their prayers
and climbed into bed.

They lay there counting bees making honey.
After almost a week, Sylvester
counted forty thousand bees.
Phyllis was already asleep, snoring.

He sighed. "Her snoring
gets louder
and louder every year.
If I don't get to sleep first,
I have to hear her snore."

For another week he listened to it.

He tied stockings
on his ears.

He paced back and forth.

He went to the kitchen and
made parsnip pancakes.

He drank hot milk
and read.

Nothing helped!
She kept snoring louder
and louder.

Outside, snowflakes blew.
Phyllis's snores made the curtains ripple
and the clock dance.

Sylvester shook her.
"If you don't stop snoring,
I can't sleep," he moaned.
"If you don't stop shaking me,
I can't sleep!" she groaned,
but fell asleep anyway.

Weeks later, Phyllis was still snoring.
Finally he wrote a note:
Dear, You snore too loud.
I will sleep somewhere else, but
I'll be back in the spring.
Love, Sylvester.

With bags under his eyes and a pillow
in his paw, Sylvester staggered off
into the woods.

Snow was piling high.
He found a hollow oak filled with
soft leaves and he climbed in.
Finally it was quiet.
The only sound he heard
was the sound of the wind.

Sylvester had such a good sleep
he slept right through spring.

Violets and skunk cabbage grew.
Noisy rabbits played outside that oak,
but Sylvester kept sleeping.

Finally the air grew warm and
flowers came into bloom.
Phyllis woke up and saw that
he was not in bed.

"Oh, he must be making coffee,"
she guessed.
However, no one was in the kitchen.

Nor under the bed,

nor in the basement,

nor in the attic.
No Sylvester anywhere!
Then she found his note.
She sat down on the front step
wondering what to do.
Somehow she had to find him.

Sylvester slept on through the summer.
Then one day a woodsman
began sawing down the oak
in which Sylvester was sleeping.
It fell to the ground with a thud.
Sylvester woke up, and looked out.

"What are you doing?
What time is it?" he asked,
still half asleep.
"I'm chopping down trees.
It's three o'clock on a
beautiful fall day,"
the woodsman answered.

"Oh my goodness!" Sylvester cried.
"I slept right through spring and summer.
Phyllis will be worried.
I must get home at once."
And he ran off through the woods.

By evening he was home.
Tall purple foxglove and goldenrod
grew all around the empty cottage.

Inside, among the soot, dust, and cobwebs,
Sylvester found a note from Phyllis.
Where are you? I waited and waited.
Now I am going out to find you. Love, Phyllis.

"I must find her at once!"
So Sylvester got on his bike and rode off
in search of Phyllis. In the distance,
he could hear the woodsman
sawing wood, and it sounded so good.
It made him think of Phyllis's snoring.
"If only I could hear her snoring
once again," he sighed.

He picked berries. And he saw her face on each berry.

He fished. And saw Phyllis's
face in the water.
As he was eating, he cried,
"Phyllis! If you were here,
it would taste better."

He rode into town.
He saw a poster for the circus.
He was still sad.
"Maybe the clowns could cheer
me up," he thought.

He bought a ticket and walked in.
He sat in the first row
to be close to the ring.
The first act was the clowns.
They made Sylvester laugh.

The next act was Rosita, the Spanish Dancer.
She danced around the ring.
Suddenly, she stopped in front of
Sylvester. She gave him a big hug.
"Get away from me, you silly bear,"
he cried, pushing her away.

"Sylvester!" she yelled.
She took off her wig and false eyelashes.
"Phyllis!" he shouted.
They hugged each other.
They sat down outside her wagon.

"I decided to join the traveling circus,
hoping to find you," she told him.
Sylvester told her about how he
had overslept in the oak and
spent months looking for her.

"That's okay," she said. "You can
sleep as long as you want."
"And *I* won't mind your snoring,"
Sylvester replied.
They went home.

That winter, Phyllis
snored louder than ever.
But Sylvester was so glad to
have her back, he just smiled
as he fell asleep.
Her snoring was music to his ears.